Welcome to ALADDIN QUIX!

If you are looking for fast, fun-to-read stories with colorful characters, lots of kid-friendly humor, easy-to-follow action, entertaining story lines, and lively illustrations, then **ALADDIN QUIX** is for you!

But wait, there's more!

If you're also looking for stories with tables of contents; word lists; about-the-book questions; 64, 80, or 96 pages; short chapters; short paragraphs; and large fonts, then **ALADDIN QUIX** is *definitely* for you!

ALADDIN QUIX: The next step between ready to reads and longer, more challenging chapter books, for readers five to eight years old.

Read more ALADDIN QUIX books!

By Stephanie Calmenson

Our Principal Is a Frog!
Our Principal Is a Wolf!
Our Principal's in His Underwear!
Our Principal Breaks a Spell!

Little Goddess Girls
By Joan Holub and Suzanne Williams

Book 1: *Athena & the Magic Land*
Book 2: *Persephone & the Giant Flowers*
Book 3: *Aphrodite & the Gold Apple*
Book 4: *Artemis & the Awesome Animals*

Mack Rhino, Private Eye

Book 1: *The Big Race Lace Case*
Book 2: *The Candy Caper Case*

Geeger the Robot

Book 1: *Geeger the Robot Goes to School*

GEEGER THE ROBOT GOES TO SCHOOL

JARRETT LERNER

Illustrated by Serge Seidlitz

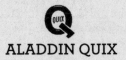

ALADDIN QUIX

New York London Toronto Sydney New Delhi

For all my teachers,
both past and present

ALADDIN QUIX
Simon & Schuster Children's Publishing Division
1230 Avenue of the Americas, New York, New York 10020
First Aladdin QUIX paperback edition August 2020
Text copyright © 2020 by Jarrett Lerner
Illustrations copyright © 2020 by Serge Seidlitz
Also available in an Aladdin QUIX hardcover edition.
All rights reserved, including the right of reproduction in whole or in part in any form.
ALADDIN and related logo are registered trademarks of Simon & Schuster, Inc.
For information about special discounts for bulk purchases, please contact
Simon & Schuster Special Sales at 1-866-506-1949 or business@simonandschuster.com.
The Simon & Schuster Speakers Bureau can bring authors to your live event. For
more information or to book an event contact the Simon & Schuster Speakers Bureau
at 1-866-248-3049 or visit our website at www.simonspeakers.com.
Book designed by Karin Paprocki
The illustrations for this book were rendered digitally.
The text of this book was set in Archer Medium.
Manufactured in the United States of America 1221 OFF
6 8 10 9 7 5
Library of Congress Control Number 2020940598
ISBN 978-1-5344-5217-6 (hardcover)
ISBN 978-1-5344-5216-9 (paperback)
ISBN 978-1-5344-5218-3 (eBook)

Cast of Characters

Geeger: a very, very hungry robot

DIGEST-O-TRON 5000: a machine that turns the food Geeger eats into electricity

Tillie: a student at Geeger's school, and Geeger's first new friend

Ms. Bork: Geeger's teacher

Arjun, Olivia, Mac, Sidney, Suzie, Gabe, Roxy, Raul: other kids in Geeger's class

Contents

Meet Geeger

Geeger is a robot. A very, very hungry robot.

That's because Geeger was built to do just one thing: **EAT!**

Geeger was **constructed** in a laboratory by a team of scientists.

Then he was sent to a town called Amblerville. There Geeger eats all the food that the rest of the **townspeople** don't want.

Like rotten eggs.

And moldy bread.

And mushy fruit.

You might say, **"YUCK!"**

But Geeger says, **"YUM."**

How does Geeger work?

Geeger has a brain, just like you. The only difference is that Geeger's brain is made up of wires.

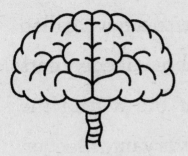

YOUR BRAIN

GEEGER'S BRAIN

Your brain, meanwhile, is made up of ... well, gooey brain stuff.

Most of the time, Geeger's brain tells him to do just one thing:

EAT! EAT! EAT! EAT! EAT!

Sometimes Geeger puts food into his mouth and chews and swallows, like you. Other times,

Geeger opens the door in his stomach and shoves the food right inside.

At the end of every day, Geeger plugs himself into his **DIGEST-O-TRON 5000.** The machine sucks up all the food that Geeger has eaten and turns it into electricity. The electricity then helps power the town!

Now and again Geeger gets confused and eats things he's not supposed to.

Like forks.

And batteries.

And toaster ovens.

When Geeger does that, the DIGEST-O-TRON lets him know. The machine's lights flash. Its sirens scream.

WEE-oOoOo!

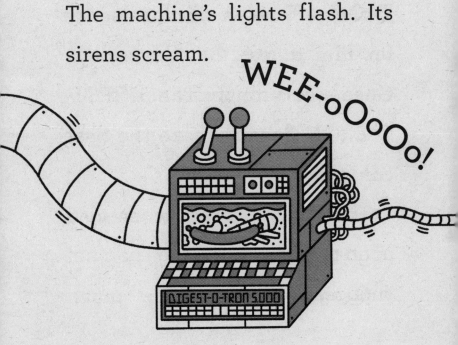

WEE-oOoOo!

WEE-oOoOo!

WEE-oOoOo!

Geeger has lived in Amblerville for one whole month. He loves it there. There's always plenty for him to eat. But some days Geeger gets lonely. The DIGEST-O-TRON doesn't make the best company.

That's why Geeger has decided to go to school!

Geeger doesn't know much

about school. In fact, he knows *nothing* about school. But it *must* be a wonderful place.

Every single morning Geeger watches all the kids in Amblerville make their way to school, and they're always laughing and smiling. School seems like the perfect place for Geeger to make a friend. Then he won't be lonely!

Geeger will soon find out if all of this is true.

Today is his first day of school!

Mostly Geeger is excited. But he's also feeling a little bit nervous.

What if he can't find his classroom?

What if he makes his teacher mad?

What if the other kids don't like him?

Geeger gives his

head a shake to knock these worries out of his wires. He **focuses**
on starting his day off right.

First he screws a brand-new
light bulb into the top of his head.
Then he goes to the kitchen,
because everyone knows that a
good day always starts with a
good breakfast—**especially
Geeger!**

2

Breakfast Time

There's no refrigerator in Geeger's kitchen. There isn't a **microwave** or an oven, either. There aren't even any tables or chairs!

Instead the room is filled with buckets and barrels and cartons

and containers of spoiled and rotten and stale and expired food.

Geeger's brain starts buzzing
as soon as he sees it all. It tells
him: **EAT! EAT! EAT! EAT!
EAT!**

So Geeger eats!

First he has:

14 eggs (rotten)

3 containers of yogurt (expired)

and

1 whole box of cereal (expired *and* stale)

"*Deee*-LISH," Geeger says, dumping the last of the cereal into his stomach. That's Robot for "delicious," which means: *yum!*

But Geeger is still hungry.

So he eats a little more:

16 bananas (brown and mushy)

7 waffles (slightly moldy)

and

1 container of motor oil (premium grade)

"Deee-LEC-TA-BLE," Geeger says, shaking the container of oil so that every last drop gets into his guts. That's Robot for

"delectable," which means: *super yummy!*

But Geeger is *still* hungry.

So he eats A LOT more:

11 more waffles (extremely moldy)

3 batteries (9-volt)

6 pieces of toast (burnt to a crisp)

2 scoops of mac and cheese (moldy)

2 scoops of mashed potatoes (even moldier)

1 backpack (stuffed full of snacks)

13 strawberries (smooshed)

22 blueberries (super smooshed)

and

2 cans of garbanzo beans (expired)

"Deee-VINE," Geeger says, tossing the second can of beans into his tummy. That's Robot for "divine," which means: *holy cow, was that yummy!*

Then Geeger checks the clock and says something else:

"UH-OH." Which is just Robot for "uh-oh," but which in this case means: *Geeger needs to hurry up and leave the house if he doesn't want to be late to school on his very first day!*

Because look at the time!

Geeger just needs to grab his backpack, and he'll be ready to go.

But where's his backpack?

Geeger thought he saw it sitting there on the counter just a moment ago. Wasn't it right between the mashed potatoes and the straw-berries?

Or maybe he left it next to the DIGEST-O-TRON. . . .

If Geeger goes to look for it, he'll *definitely* be late for school.

What's worse: showing up late on your very first day of school, or showing up without a backpack?

Geeger checks his other clock.

Eek!

Before he can waste another second, Geeger hurries out the door.

3

Meet Tillie

Outside, the sidewalks are already crowded with kids on their way to school.

There are big kids, little kids, and in-between-size kids. Most of them walk, but some ride bikes, and a few **swerve** in and out of the others on skateboards.

Geeger can't help but notice that every last one of the kids is wearing a backpack.

As he joins the kids, a **strange** feeling fills Geeger's stomach. It's like a bunch of butterflies somehow snuck in there and are now flapping around like crazy.

Geeger steps aside and stops. He opens the door to his stomach and peers inside.

There's the problem!

Sitting among the rotten eggs and mushy bananas and moldy mashed potatoes is...*his backpack!*

"PHEW!" Geeger says.

He pulls out his backpack and closes the door to his stomach.

He's about to step back onto the sidewalk when he notices that someone is standing in his way.

It's a girl. She has curly hair and bright eyes and a big smile. She's staring right up at Geeger.

"Hi!" she says. "What's your name?"

"GEE-GER," Geeger says.

"Geeger?" says the girl. "I've never heard that name before."

Geeger worries that this is a bad thing. But then the girl says,

"How cool! I'm **Tillie.** Something about me you should probably know—I'm *really* good at jump rope."

Geeger doesn't know what jump rope is. But since Tillie is

so proud of her jump rope skills, he says, **"COOL."**

Tillie says, "Yesterday I did forty-two jumps in a row!"

Geeger says, **"YES-TER-DAY I ATE FOR-TY TWO SLI-CES OF MOL-DY** *cheeese***."**

Tillie giggles.

"You're funny," she tells Geeger. Then, without a word of warning, she spins around and zips off down the street.

Geeger watches her go.

"COOL, COOL," he says, **experimenting** with this brand-new word. *"Cooooool."*

Geeger hasn't even gotten to school yet, and he's already learning!

4

Brand-New Student

Geeger's school is bigger than he thought it would be.

There are so many different hallways, and they all look exactly the same. And there are even more doors. There must be more than a hundred of them!

Luckily, all the doors have signs on them, so Geeger has no

problem finding his classroom.

As he stands outside his class-room door, that butterfly feeling starts up in Geeger's stomach again.

But Geeger doesn't have time to look and see what *else* he accidentally ate for breakfast. **Class is about to start!**

Geeger steps into the room and looks around. There are desks and chairs and lots and lots of kids.

Some kids are talking. Others draw or read. Along the walls of the room are bookshelves, which are crammed full of more books than Geeger ever knew **existed**.

Standing at the front of the

room is a woman with short hair and a skirt decorated with pictures of even *more* books.

Geeger knows this must be his teacher, **Ms. Bork**. She looks nice. Geeger really, really hopes he doesn't do anything to make her mad.

Just then, Ms. Bork sees Geeger. She smiles and waves him up to the front of the classroom.

Geeger goes, his stomach fluttering.

"Class," Ms. Bork says once Geeger is standing beside her. "Please find your seats."

The kids get quiet. They put away their papers and books, and sit down at their desks.

Toward the back of the room, Geeger spots someone **familiar**—Tillie! Seeing her makes Geeger feel a little less nervous.

"We have a brand-new student joining our class today," Ms. Bork says. "Please say hello to Geeger."

"Hello, Geeger!" the kids

all say.

Geeger raises a hand and wiggles

his fingers. **"HEL-LO,** *ki-i-ids."*

"Now, Geeger," says Ms. Bork. "Would you care to tell us all a bit more about yourself, and just what you came to our town of Amblerville to do?"

Geeger looks out at his class-mates. Every single one of them is staring up at him, waiting for him to speak.

And the way Geeger's stom-ach feels at this moment, it's like he accidentally ate *two hundred backpacks.*

Geeger wants to run out the door and all the way back home. But before he can, Tillie catches his eye. She gives him a grin and a big thumbs-up.

Geeger smiles back. Then he opens his mouth and tells the kids all about himself.

5

Bells and Whistles

Geeger begins by saying: **"I AM A RO-BOT."** Then he tells the kids, "A RO-BOT BUILT TO *ea-a-at*."

Next he tells them *what* he eats: all the spoiled and rotten and stale and **expired** food that the kids and their families don't want.

"Ew!" says a kid named **Arjun**.

At the same time, a girl named **Olivia** says, **"Awesome!"**

Geeger doesn't understand how something can be gross and awesome at the same time. But the kids all seem interested in what he has to say, so he keeps on sharing.

He tells the kids about the DIGEST-O-TRON 5000, and how it

turns all the food he eats into elec-tricity, which then helps power the town's lights and computers and refrigerators and TVs.

Next Geeger tells the kids about the wires that make up his brain.

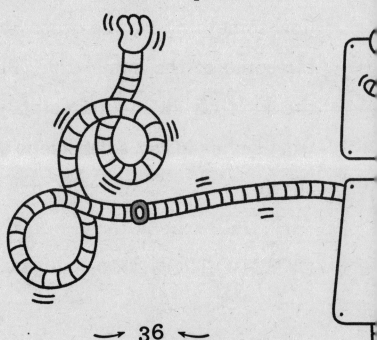

At last he says, **"AL-SO, I HAVE SOME BELLS** *aaand* **WHISTLES."**

Geeger shows the kids how his super stretchy arms can reach all the way from one side of the room to the other.

"Amazing!" says **Mac**.

Sidney says, "So cool!"

Then Geeger shows the kids how, if he pokes out his leg just right, he can pick up radio stations and play music.

"I know that song!" says **Suzie**.

Gabe says, "It's my favorite!"

Finally Geeger shows the kids the *actual* bells and whistles that he keeps in a compartment in his side.

"Nifty!" says **Roxy**.

Raul says, "*So* cool!"

Geeger feels like he's on top of the world. No—like he's on top of the *universe*!

Tillie gives him a grin and a *double* thumbs-up.

"Thank you, Geeger," says Ms. Bork. "We are so excited to have you in our class. Now, as the rest of you know, we'll be starting our day with a geography lesson."

Ms. Bork steps over to her desk. She moves aside a few books and pencils.

Then Ms. Bork picks up an **object** Geeger has never seen before.

It's big and round and blue, and covered in some sort of greenish-brown crusty stuff.

To Geeger it looks like a giant piece of moldy blue fruit. And that's when Geeger's brain starts buzzing.

EAT! EAT! EAT! EAT! EAT!

Geeger snatches the globe—because that's what the object *really* is—out of Ms. Bork's hand. Then he quickly crams it into his mouth.

Olivia gasps.

Arjun yelps.

Ms. Bork **gapes** at her now-empty hands.

"Um," she says. "I—I guess we can skip right to making our maps. . . ."

Back at her desk Ms. Bork pulls open a drawer and takes out a bin. In the bin are a bunch of long, thin, colorful **cylinders**, plus several tubes of something thick and white.

EAT! EAT! EAT! EAT! EAT!

Geeger grabs the colored pencils first. But before he can get his hands on a single tube of glue, Ms. Bork yanks the bin away from him.

Geeger looks up at her. And the expression on her face is not a good one. If Ms. Bork were a DIGEST-O-TRON 5000, her lights would be flashing and her sirens would be screaming.

WEE-oOoOo!

WEE-oOoOo!

WEE-oOoOo!

Geeger is confused.

Things were going so well.

What happened?

"Class," Ms. Bork says, never once taking her eyes off Geeger. "You may go to recess early. Geeger and I need to have a talk."

Making Mistakes

Geeger watches the kids file out of the classroom. Tillie is the last to leave. She glances back at the last second and gives Geeger a worried look.

"Geeger?"

It's Ms. Bork. She holds a hand out to an empty desk, asking Geeger to sit.

Geeger squeezes into the chair and looks up at his teacher.

"I AM IN TROU-BLE?" he asks.

"No," says Ms. Bork. "You're just learning. You see, there are some things that it might be okay to do at home but that it's *not* okay to do at school."

Geeger has a scary thought.

"THERE IS NO EAT-ING IN

schoo-oo-ool?" he asks Ms. Bork.

Ms. Bork smiles.

"You can eat at snack time," she says. "And during lunch, in the cafeteria. But you'll also have to learn what you are and are *not* supposed to eat."

"I WAS NOT SUP-POSED TO EAT BIG BLUE MOL-DY FRUIT?" Geeger asks.

"That," says Ms. Bork, "was a *globe*. And no, you were *not* supposed to eat it."

Geeger wriggles around in his seat so that he can open the door to his stomach.

He reaches a hand into his guts and pulls out Ms. Bork's globe. One side of it is a bit dented. There's a gob of moldy mac and cheese stuck to North America.

But it looks like the globe can be cleaned and fixed up, good as new.

Ms. Bork carries the globe over to her desk.

Geeger points to the object she sets the globe next to.

"THAT IS NOT BIG PIECE OF BURNT TOAST?" he asks.

Ms. Bork lifts up the object. "This," she says, "is my note-book. It has a leather cover."

Geeger points to something else. **"THAT IS NOT A SHI-NY DOUGH-NUT?"** he asks.

"That," says Ms. Bork, "is a roll of **duct tape**."

Geeger sighs. **"THIS IS VE-RY CON-FUS-ING."**

"That's okay, Geeger," says Ms. Bork. "Everyone gets confused sometimes."

Geeger eyes his teacher. "**EV-EN MS. BORK?**"

"*Especially* Ms. Bork," says Ms. Bork, smiling. "There's no reason to be embarrassed about getting confused."

Geeger understands what Ms. Bork is saying. But he's not sure he will be able to ignore his brain when it tells him to **EAT! EAT! EAT! EAT! EAT!** It's going to be hard. *Really* hard. But if Geeger wants to stay in school—and he *does*—he's going to have to try.

"You might continue to make mistakes," Ms. Bork tells Geeger. "And that's okay too. Mistakes are chances to learn, Geeger—some of the best chances there are."

"O-KAY," Geeger says. **"I WILL TRY MY BEST."**

"That's perfect," Ms. Bork says. "Now come on. I'll show you how to get to the playground for recess."

7

A Spaghetti Strand

Ms. Bork leads Geeger outside.

"I **realize** this is all very new to you," she tells him. "I'll try to be better about explaining things. I'll start right now."

First Ms. Bork points to the

long patch of pavement that has the tall metal poles at either end.

"That's a basketball court," Ms. Bork says, and then she explains how the game is played.

Next she points to a row of big plastic tubes.

"Those are tunnels. You can crawl through them, from one side to the other."

Then Ms. Bork points to one more big plastic tube, but this one is angled upward and has stairs leading to the higher side.

"And that," she says, "is a slide. You climb to the top, then *sli-i-ide* down to the bottom."

"BAS-KET-BALL COURT," Geeger repeats. **"TUN-NELS AND** *sliiide*."

"You got it!" Ms. Bork says. "Now, is it okay if I go back inside?"

Geeger **hesitates**. He would much rather Ms. Bork *not* go back inside. It would be easier if she were there next to him during recess. She could stop him from doing anything he's not supposed to.

Ms. Bork sets a hand on Geeger's shoulder. "You can do this," she tells him. "I know you can."

With that, Ms. Bork goes back into the school.

But Geeger isn't alone for long.

"Hey, Geeger! Over here!"

It's Tillie. She's standing in one corner of the basketball court with Arjun, Olivia, and Raul.

Geeger makes his way over to them.

"Is everything okay?" Tillie asks when he arrives.

Geeger opens his mouth to tell the kids what he and Ms. Bork just spoke about—but it's at that very moment that Geeger finally sees what Tillie is holding in her hands.

It's a long yellow rope. . . .

It's a giant strand of spaghetti!

Geeger's brain starts buzzing.

EAT! EAT! EAT! EAT! EAT!

The next thing Geeger knows, his hand shoots out and snatches the spaghetti.

EAT! EAT! EAT! EAT! EAT!

Geeger brings the spaghetti to his mouth.

EAT! EAT! *Eeeeeeeee—*

All of a sudden there's a new

word buzzing through Geeger's

brain:

STOP!

Geeger lowers the spaghetti.

The kids are all staring up at

him. Tillie looks confused. Arjun and Olivia and Raul look confused *and* scared.

"TIL-LIE," Geeger says. "THIS IS SPA-GHET-*teee*?"

Tillie blinks. Then she grins.

"That's my jump rope!" Tillie says, giggling.

She takes the jump rope back from Geeger and hands one end to Arjun. On the count of three, Tillie and Arjun start whipping the rope around. Then Olivia and Raul race in and take turns hopping over the rope.

Geeger stands back and watches. Then he gets an idea.

Geeger pokes out his leg, and music starts to play.

Soon all the other kids from Ms. Bork's class run over to jump rope with their new friend—Geeger the robot!

8

Learning

Later that day during lunch, Geeger eats a plastic spoon. Also a ball of aluminum foil.

But then he makes it through the whole rest of the day at school without eating a single thing he's not supposed to!

Geeger knows he's not done making mistakes.

Speaking of which, back at home later that day:

WEE-oOoOo!

WEE-oOoOo!

WEE-oOoOo!

Geeger opens his stomach and peers inside. He removes the batteries he must have stuck in there earlier, during breakfast. Then he reaches for a rag and sops up a puddle of what looks like motor oil.

"SOR-*reee*, DI-GEST-O-TRON," Geeger tells the machine.

He closes his stomach. Then he closes his eyes. But before he drifts off to sleep, Geeger tells the DIGEST-O-TRON one more thing:

"BUT I AM LEARN-ING."

Word List

constructed (con•STRUHK•ted):
Built

cylinders (SILL•en•duhrs): Round,
tube-like shapes with closed ends

duct tape (DUCKT TAYP): A
strong tape used to fix heating
and air-conditioning units

existed (ik•SIS•ted): Lived or was
alive

**experimenting (ik•SPEHR•i•ment•
ing):** Trying something out

expired (ik•SPY•ehrd): Came to
an end

familiar (FUH•mill•yer): Known;
seen before

focuses (FO•cuhs•ehs): Pays
close attention to

gapes (GAYPS): Stares with
one's mouth open in surprise
and/or amazement

hesitates (HEH•zih•tayts):
Pauses

microwave (MY•croh•wayv): An
oven that heats up food quickly

object (ahb•JEKT): A thing that can be seen and touched

realize (REE•uh•lize): Understand completely

strange (STRAYNJ): Unusual; never before seen

swerve (SWURV): Move quickly back and forth

townspeople (TOWNS•pee• puhl): Grown-ups and kids who live in a particular city

Questions

1. Geeger is both excited and nervous about his first day of school. Do you remember your first day of school? How did you feel?

2. How does Geeger lose his backpack? When does he find it?

3. Tillie is proud of her jump-rope skills. What is a skill that you are proud of having?

4. Why does Ms. Bork send her class to recess early? Why does she ask Geeger to stay behind?

5. Ms. Bork says that mistakes are chances to learn. Have you ever made a mistake? Did you learn something from it?

6. Geeger learns lots of things during his first day of school. List as many as you can.